UNLOVABLE

Dan Yaccarino

Henry Holt and Company • **New York**

This book is for my buddy Alfred.

Henry Holt and Company, LLC, *Publishers since 1866*
175 Fifth Avenue, New York, New York 10010 [www.HenryHoltKids.com]

Henry Holt® **is a registered trademark of Henry Holt and Company, LLC.**
Copyright © 2001 by Dan Yaccarino. All rights reserved.
Distributed in Canada by H. B. Fenn and Company Ltd.

Library of Congress Cataloging-in-Publication Data
Yaccarino, Dan. Unlovable / Dan Yaccarino.
Summary: Alfred, a pug, is made to feel inferior by a cat, a parrot, and the other neighborhood dogs,
until a new dog moves in next door and helps Alfred to realize he is just fine the way he is.
[1. Pug—Fiction.   2. Dogs—Fiction.   3. Self-perception—Fiction.   4. Friendship—Fiction.]   I. Title.
PZ7.Y125Un   2001   [E]—dc21   00-47299

First published in hardcover in 2001 by Henry Holt and Company
First paperback edition—2004 / Designed by Dan Yaccarino and Donna Mark
The artist used gouache on watercolor paper to create the illustrations for this book.

ISBN 978-0-8050-6321-9 (hardcover)
5 7 9 10 8 6 4
ISBN 978-0-8050-7532-8 (paperback)
5 7 9 10 8 6

Printed in March 2010 in China by South China Printing Company Ltd.,
Dongguan City, Guangdong Province, on acid-free paper. ∞

Alfred was unlovable.

At least that's what the cat told him every chance he got.

"You've got the *ugliest* mug I've ever seen. *No one* could love you!"

Alfred tried his best to ignore the remarks, but it was difficult, especially since the cat had taught the parrot to say "Unlovable! *Squawk!* Unlovable!" whenever Alfred walked by. The goldfish gurgled in agreement.

But what was it that made him unlovable?

His snoring?

The way that he ate?

His little curly tail?

None of the neighborhood dogs would have a thing to do with him.

"His mouth is too small to hold a ball," a big German shepherd sneered.

"His legs are way too short for running," snickered a greyhound.

A pampered poodle chuckled. "Did you see that face?"

"Beat it, shrimp," growled a Doberman.

"You couldn't even scare a mailman."

Alfred didn't like staying in the house since the cat was always making fun of him, the parrot was always squawking "Unlovable!" and the goldfish was always gurgling in agreement. So Alfred spent most of his time alone in the backyard.

One day a new family moved in next door. Alfred tried to see if they had a dog who might be his friend, but he was too little to look over the fence.

As he was sniffing around, he heard something on the other side.

"Hello?" Alfred called.

"Hi," came the answer. "I'm Rex. I just moved in."

"My name is Alfred." And, without thinking, he blurted out, "I'm a golden retriever."

"Glad to meet you," Rex replied.

Alfred and Rex talked for hours. Alfred said he liked sleeping in the sun, dog food, and scratching. Rex did too. Rex said he hated baths and going to the vet. Alfred did too.

It began to get dark. Soon it was time for dinner, and they both went inside. That night Alfred thought about how much he liked Rex and how much they had in common. Then he thought about the fib he had told. Alfred was sure they'd be friends—as long as Rex never saw how unlovable he was.

The next day when Alfred and Rex were chatting, a squirrel jumped onto the fence between them. They both barked at it. The squirrel took one look at Alfred and climbed up a tree.

Rex said, "You sure showed that squirrel who's boss, Alfred."

But Alfred was thinking, *If Rex ever sees me he'll run away too.*

"I'm going to dig a hole under the fence,"
Rex said one day. "Then I can squeeze through
to your side, and we can meet."

Alfred heard Rex digging. When he heard Rex
wiggle under the fence, he ran and hid behind a bush.
Then he heard Rex call, "Alfred, where are you?"

Suddenly Rex poked his head into the bush where Alfred was hiding.

"Y-you look just like me!" gasped Alfred.
"Wow! This is great," said Rex. "You're not
a golden retriever after all!"

Alfred had to laugh. Who cared what
the others said? Rex was his friend, and
Rex liked him just the way he was.

Together Alfred and Rex ran.

They jumped.

They played.

And Alfred never felt unlovable again.